MW01017559

The School Play

Adapted by Meredith Rusu

SCHOLASTIC INC.

ISBN 978-1-338-21027-9

10 9 8 7 6 5 4 3   18 19 20 21 22
Printed in the U.S.A.   40

First printing 2018
Book design by Jessica Meltzer

Peppa Pig is very excited today.

Her class is putting on
a school play!

The play is called
Little Red Riding Hood.
All the children
will be in the play.

Peppa will play the part of Little Red Riding Hood.

Danny Dog will be the Big Bad Wolf.

Rebecca Rabbit will be
the grandma.

Pedro Pony will be the hunter.

Mrs. Pony helps Pedro
practice his lines.

He will save Little Red Riding
Hood from the Big Bad Wolf.

Peppa must practice, too.
"I am Little Red Riding Hood!"
she says. "I am going to visit
my grandma."

"Very good!" says Daddy Pig.
Peppa likes acting!

Soon, it is the big day.
"Welcome to our play!"
says Madame Gazelle.

"First, let us meet the actors."
All the children go on stage.

The play begins.
Danny pretends to be
the Big Bad Wolf.

"Go in the closet!" Danny tells
Rebecca.
   He is going to wait for
Little Red Riding Hood.

Now Peppa comes on stage.

"I am Little Red Riding Hood,"
she says.

Peppa pretends to walk
through the woods.
"I am going to visit my grandma."

Peppa is very good at acting
like Little Red Riding Hood.

Peppa is at Grandma's house.
"Oh! You do not look like
my grandma," she tells Danny.

"What big eyes you have.
What big teeth you have.
You are not Grandma!
You are the Big Bad Wolf!"

"Help!" cries Peppa.
It is Pedro's turn
to come on stage.
But Pedro is shy.

Madame Gazelle comes
with him.
That makes him feel better.
"Go away, you Big Bad Wolf!"
says Pedro.

Hooray! Pedro has saved
Little Red Riding Hood from
the Big Bad Wolf.

The play is over.

"Bravo!" say all the parents.
They clap and cheer.

They take lots of pictures.
Everyone is very proud.

Peppa and her friends take a bow.

They all did a good job acting!

"Pedro, you were very good,"
says Peppa. "You were almost
as good as me!"

Hee, hee!
"Thank you, Peppa!" says Pedro.

Peppa is glad she was
in the school play.
She hopes there will be
another one soon!